THE FAMOUS FIVE
SHORT STORIES

TIMMY AND THE TREASURE

The Famous Five

Timmy   George   Julian   Dick   Anne

HODDER CHILDREN'S BOOKS

First published in Great Britain in 2022 by Hodder & Stoughton

1 3 5 7 9 10 8 6 4 2

The Famous Five®, Enid Blyton® and Enid Blyton's signature
are registered trade marks of Hodder & Stoughton Limited
Written by Sufiya Ahmed. Text © 2022 Hodder & Stoughton Limited
Illustrations by Becka Moor. Illustrations © 2022 Hodder & Stoughton Limited

A CIP catalogue record for this book is available from the British Library.

ISBN 978 1 444 96006 8

Printed and bound in China
The paper and board used in this book are made from wood from responsible sources.

Hodder Children's Books
An imprint of
Hachette Children's Group
Part of Hodder & Stoughton
Carmelite House
50 Victoria Embankment
London EC4Y 0DZ

An Hachette UK Company
www.hachette.co.uk
www.hachettechildrens.co.uk

Enid Blyton

TIMMY AND THE TREASURE

illustrated by **Becka Moor**

written by **Sufiya Ahmed**

HODDER

Famous Five Colour Short Stories

For a complete list of the full-length
Famous Five adventures, turn to
the last page of this book

CONTENTS

CHAPTER ONE

Aunt Fanny placed a pot of tea on the table.
'Children, would you like to help out a friend of mine?'

George glanced up from the jam she was spreading on her toast and looked at her cousins, **Julian, Dick and Anne,** who were **hungrily** tucking into their breakfast. She was pleased they were spending the last few weeks of summer **together,** even if she didn't always admit it. **'What's that, Mother?'** she said as she fed the toast to Timmy under the table.

'A friend from my book club needs some help,' Aunt Fanny explained. 'It's Mrs Tidyworth, who lives in the big house at the **top of the cliff**. She wants to create a little public garden up there in **honour** of her late husband. **Do you remember him, George?'**

George nodded. Mr Tidyworth had been **very funny and jolly,** and had been known by his nickname, **Tidy.**

Aunt Fanny helped herself to a slice of toast. 'Can I count on you all to help?'

'Yes!' Julian said, deciding for them.

'Oh, good,' Aunt Fanny said, looking relieved. 'The project will keep you all occupied and **out of trouble**. Finish your breakfast, and **I'll pack you a picnic lunch.'**

The **long walk** up to the clifftop made them **hungry** and they **all agreed** that an **early lunch was a good idea.**

Soon Timmy was **licking** the last of the crumbs off the blanket.

The children had just enjoyed **cheese and pickle sandwiches, boiled eggs** and **cake,** all washed down with **ginger beer.**

Now they were **ready** to work on their **plans** for the garden. There was already an area **fenced off** for it.

'Let's get started,' Julian said, unrolling some paper from his satchel. He weighted down the edges with pebbles he found on the ground.

He **twirled a pencil** between his fingers. 'So what shall I include in my sketch?'

'A garden needs **flowers** and I'd like to organise them,' Anne said. 'I know **just** the **type and colour** to plant.'

'How about a **climbing frame?**' George suggested. 'And a **slide** and **swings**?'

'Draw a **play area** for George,' Dick teased with a grin.

'It's called an **adventure park!**' George retorted.

10

'OK, OK,' Dick laughed, before neatly catching the tape measure Julian threw at him. 'Come on, George, hold one end and walk over to that fence. We need to **measure** the place first.'

CHAPTER TWO

Hours later the Five **trudged** home, **tired but satisfied.** They now knew **exactly** how the garden was going to look.

Aunt Fanny called out to them from the

kitchen. **'Can you all come here, please? I'd like you to meet someone.'**

George recognised the old lady at the table. 'Oh, hello, **Mrs Tidyworth.**'

'Hello, dear Georgina. **Oh, my,** you've grown since the last time I saw you.'

'Please don't call me that,' George started to say, but was almost **drowned out** by the noise of Timmy **bounding up, barking** and **wagging his tail.**

'Well, hello there.' Mrs Tidyworth patted Timmy's head. **'Aren't you friendly?** And these must be your cousins, George. It's very nice to meet you all. Fanny told me about your offer to **help** with the garden.'

'**Yes!**' Anne said excitedly, **clapping her hands**. 'I've planned the flower bed. We're going to have **red and white roses.**'

Mrs Tidyworth's eyes took on a faraway look. 'Oh, my. **Tidy loved flowers.** He liked **tulips, carnations, pansies, foxgloves, snowdrops, daffodils, hollyhocks and roses too.** And those are just the ones I can remember off the top of my head.'

Anne blinked. '**Oh.**'

'May we show you our ideas?' Julian asked, pulling out a chair.

He rolled his plan out on the table and guided Mrs Tidyworth through the sketch. 'This is the **entrance.** We'll have a **lawn area** here and a **sandpit** here . . .'

'Don't forget the **climbing apparatus,'** George interrupted.

'Yes, I'm getting to that. This area is for the **climbing frame** and **Anne's flowers** will be planted all around **here.'**

'This all looks **very impressive**,' Aunt Fanny remarked, 'but who is going to pay for it all? I imagine it will cost quite a bit.'

The children turned to her with **surprised faces.**

She looked apologetic. 'I should have mentioned that. I suppose I didn't realise you would go in with **full force.**'

'Mother, when have you **ever** known us to do things by halves?' George demanded.

Julian turned back to Mrs Tidyworth.
'Why don't you tell us what you had in mind?'

'I was hoping to plant some **flowers,**' she admitted. 'Maybe add a few **pot plants** and a **bench** with a **plaque** that reads **"TIDY'S GARDEN"**. That's all the money I can spare.'

'We can do that for you,' Julian said brightly. 'We'll just need to clear some weeds for the planting.'

'Yes, we love digging,' Dick said. 'Especially Timmy. Don't you, boy?'

'Woof,' Timmy barked.

CHAPTER THREE

The Five set off the next morning armed with **gardening equipment** and **seed packets.** It was a **sunny** day and, after **digging out** weeds **all morning,** by noon they were all feeling the **heat.**

'Let's take a break,' Dick said, **leaning** on his gardening rake.

Anne dropped her spade. **'Good idea.'**

The children **sprawled on the ground** and **gulped down their ginger beer,** enjoying **every drop.**

Dick **squinted** into the sun.

'What's Timmy up to?'

The others turned to see Timmy

burrowing down in one spot.

'Here, boy!' George called.

Timmy looked up. **'Woof,'** he barked, and then he carried on with **gusto.**

'You're making a mess,' Anne scolded. 'This is meant to be a **tidy garden.'**

Timmy ignored her and kept **digging,** creating an **ever-growing pile of earth.**

'I think he's **found** something,' George said, getting down on **all fours** to peer into the hole.

'Probably some **rubbish** from a **shipwreck,**' Julian said rather dismissively.

George **jumped** back to her feet.

30

'Shipwrecks are found on the **beach** by the sea, **not high up on clifftops** and ... **Oh!**' She looked down as Timmy pulled out a **small drawstring bag,** covered in mud. He **dropped** it **at her feet.**

'**Wait!**' Julian commanded, scrambling up. '**I'll open it.**'

'Why do you get to do it?' George demanded. 'Timmy found it and he's **my** dog.'

Julian and George were so busy **glaring** at each other that they failed to notice Dick **swoop** in. **'Too late!'**

'**Hey!**' Julian and George exclaimed, **hands on hips.**

'**Just open it!**' Anne urged from behind them.

Dick **pulled** the string and **peered** inside. 'I can see something.'

'What is it?' Anne could barely contain her excitement.

'**It's . . .**' Dick tentatively put his hand inside and felt around.

'If you don't . . .' But George's words dried up as Dick pulled his hand out and they all stared at an object that **gleamed in the sun.**

Anne gasped. **'Is that a silver necklace?'**

CHAPTER FOUR

The children **hurried** round to see Mrs
Tidyworth and were soon sitting in her garden,
sipping **lemonade.**

'Isn't it lovely?' said Anne. 'It was

a bit **dirty,** but Dick cleaned it with his handkerchief.'

Mrs Tidyworth peered at the necklace through her glasses. 'I think I know who this belonged to. **Follow me.'**

She led them into the house and to a **painting** in the hallway. It was a portrait of a **stern-looking** woman. 'That's my husband's **great-great-grandmother,** Juliette Tidyworth. **Look closely.'**

'Oh!' Anne exclaimed. 'She's wearing the necklace.'

'Indeed!'

'So it belongs to your family?' Julian asked. 'It didn't come off a shipwreck?'

George rolled her eyes. **'I already**

told you that!' she muttered. She turned to Mrs Tidyworth. **'But who buried it? And why?'**

Suddenly Dick slumped back against the portrait and buried his face in his hands. **'Oh, no!** Maybe it was **cursed** and the necklace had to be **buried** to end **bad luck.'** He peeped out through his fingers. **'And I touched it!'**

The others looked away, their lips **twitching** with laughter. Dick loved to make jokes.

'You may be right,' Mrs Tidyworth said gravely. 'A **terrible curse** was laid on the **Juliette necklace.** It was said that **whoever touched it** would wake to find **worms** crawling over them in the night.'

Dick's hands and face fell. 'Wha—'

Then he saw the **twinkle** in Mrs Tidyworth's eyes. He sighed with **relief** as the others all started to laugh at him.

Mrs Tidyworth smiled. 'I had no idea the necklace had gone missing. We all thought that it must have been sold a **long time ago** because Juliette was the **last** Tidyworth to wear it.'

'Does it feel nice to have it after all this time?' Anne asked.

'It does,' Mrs Tidyworth replied, walking slowly towards the kitchen. 'And I think Timmy deserves a **treat** for his **discovery.**'

Timmy's ears **pricked up.** He had just heard his **favourite** word.

The next day Aunt Fanny asked the children to **visit Mrs Tidyworth** again. 'She has a favour to ask and I've already given my permission.'

They waited with **bated breath** to hear more.

'She can tell you herself,' Aunt Fanny said **mysteriously.**

The suspense was enough to make the four children **gulp** down their breakfast and hurry to the big house.

'I telephoned an **antique dealer** in Hopperton yesterday afternoon,' Mrs Tidyworth explained. 'He thinks the necklace could be **very valuable** and wants to see it. May I ask **you** to make the trip for me? I can provide the **train tickets.** If you leave **now,** you can make it there and back before **supper.'**

In no time the **Five** were sitting in a train carriage heading for **Hopperton.** Timmy tucked himself under the table, **guarding the food basket** that Mrs Tidyworth had prepared for them. He would make sure they **didn't forget** it when they got off the train!

CHAPTER FIVE

The train pulled to a stop just as a **cat** jumped down from a railing to stroll leisurely along the platform.

Timmy **spotted** her just as Julian opened the carriage door. **'Woof!'**

Before any of the children could stop him, Timmy had **bolted** after the cat.

Passengers **bumped** and **tripped** over each other to avoid the **great chase.**

'Timmy! No!' George cried.

The children **rushed** after Timmy as
the **terrified cat** led them up steep
roads and down alleyways before **finally
disappearing** over a high wall.

'**Grrr,**' Timmy **growled** quietly in frustration.

The children leaned against the bricks, **struggling** to catch their breath. **'That was naughty, Timmy!'** George panted.

Then Julian groaned, feeling his jacket pocket. **'Oh, no! I've lost the necklace!'**

'What?' Dick, Anne and George cried in unison.

'The envelope with the necklace must have **fallen out** of my pocket when we were **chasing** Timmy,' he said.

'What are we going to do?' Anne asked in horror.

Dick straightened up. 'Let's **retrace our steps.**'

Heads bent, the four children **scoured** the ground along the route they'd run. They were nearly back at the station when Timmy suddenly **dived off** the pavement.

'Woof,' he barked, his nose almost hidden behind a car wheel.

'**Hurray!**' George said as the dog's head popped back into view with the envelope in his jaw. '**Timmy saves the day again.**'

Julian **scowled.** 'If he hadn't chased that cat in the first place—'

'We'll be late,' Anne interrupted before her cousin and brother could argue any more. '**Let's go.**'

The bell over the door **rang** as Julian, Dick and Anne walked into the antique shop. The window had a sign that read **NO DOGS ALLOWED**, so George and Timmy were waiting outside.

'Everything is **so old**,' Anne marvelled, looking around.

Her brothers laughed. 'That's why they're called **antiques!'**

'Are you the children from **Kirrin Village?'** a man asked from behind the counter.

'We are,' said Julian, and he carefully handed over the envelope.

They waited **patiently** as the antique dealer **examined** the necklace.

'Well,' he said at long last. 'This is **extremely valuable.** It's not silver but **white gold,** and it's **beautifully made.** You had better be careful **not** to **lose** it on your way home.'

The children **gulped.** Thank
goodness he didn't know what had happened
before they got to his shop!

The next morning the children went down to breakfast to find Mrs Tidyworth already seated at the kitchen table.

'I **couldn't wait** to share the news,' she said, **beaming.** 'The dealer telephoned me first thing this morning. He offered to buy the necklace for a **considerable sum** and I've accepted.'

'Don't you want to **keep it** in your family?' Anne asked. 'It's very pretty.'

'I don't have any children to pass it on to,' Mrs Tidyworth replied. 'It's a **mystery** to me why the necklace ended up **buried for decades,** but I feel the place where it was found should now **benefit** from it.'

'What do you mean?'
George asked.

'The money is more than enough to make your **garden plans** come true,' Mrs Tidyworth said with a smile. 'Julian, would you please **dig out your sketch?** I think we need to make a **list** of **all** the things we need to **buy.**'

CHAPTER SIX

The garden was finally ready for its **grand opening,** complete with a plaque on the bench reading **TIDY'S GARDEN.**

Aunt Fanny **gazed** at the riot of colour in the flower beds. 'I thought you wanted **red**

and white roses, Anne?'

'Mrs Tidyworth said Tidy loved **all sorts** of flowers, so I thought we should include as many **different** ones as possible.'

Aunt Fanny patted Anne's back. 'I think that was a **very** good idea. **Oh, look,** it's time for the speeches.'

A moment later the Five stood at the
front of the crowd as Mrs Tidyworth **beamed**
at the **large gathering** of Kirrin villagers.

'My husband, **Tidy,** **loved people** and he **loved the outdoors,**' she said. 'He would want you **all** to enjoy this garden, so **please visit whenever you want.**

'I would like to thank **Julian, Dick, George** and **Anne** for **helping me** complete the project, and **especially Timmy.** If it wasn't for his **special investigative digging skills,** we might not be surrounded by all this.'

'**Three cheers for Timmy!** Hip, hip . . .' Dick cried.

'**Hurrah!**' the crowd cheered.

Timmy wagged his tail and George looked as if she might **burst** with pride.

If you enjoyed this Famous Five short story, there's plenty more action and adventure in the full-length Famous Five novels. Here is a list of all the titles, in the order they were first published.